For my daughter, Lily—
my star, forever

First edition 2006

Library of Congress Cataloging-in-Publication Data is available.

Library of Congress Catalog Number 2005053185

ISBN 0-7636-2914-6

2 4 6 8 10 9 7 5 3 1

Printed in China

This book was typeset in Maiandra.
The illustrations were done in pencil, ink, and acrylic.

Candlewick Press
2067 Massachusetts Avenue
Cambridge, Massachusetts 02140

visit us at www.candlewick.com

STAR OF THE WEEK

BARNEY SALTZBERG

CANDLEWICK PRESS

CAMBRIDGE, MASSACHUSETTS

When Stanley Birdbaum heard the news,
he practically flew home from school.

"I'm star of the week!" he shouted.
"It's my turn to share my favorite things."

That night Stanley and his mom prepared snacks.
"They're going to love this!" he said.

"You're my star every day!" said Stanley's mom
as he left for school the next morning.

In class, Mr. Winger pinned a star to Stanley's shirt.

"I'm sure everyone would like a little snack," he said.
"Did you bring your favorite food?"

Stanley passed around sandwiches. "They're tofu bologna, cream cheese, and jelly with pickles," he told them. "On pumpernickel!"

Stanley was happily nibbling his sandwich when he noticed that no one else was eating.

"They're good!" he assured everyone. "Really!"

Mr. Winger took a bite. "I've never had tofu bologna, cream cheese, and jelly with pickles before," he said. "Pickles do add a nice texture!"

"I'm not eating this!" said Polly Seedeater.
"It's disgusting!"

I thought this was going to be fun, Stanley
said to himself. I think I was wrong!

As star of the week,
Stanley also got to
share his favorite toy.

At home,
he tried to
pick one.

It took a while.

"I know today will be better," said Stanley's mom
as he left for school the next morning.

When it was time for Stanley to share his favorite toy, he pulled a plastic robot out of his bag.

"Is that a *doll*?" Polly Seedeater asked.

Everybody laughed.

"This is Mr. Bizzo," said Stanley.
"He's a walking, talking robot."

Stanley wound Mr. Bizzo up. "Hello, hello, hello!"
the robot repeated as it rolled across the floor. Then
Boing! An arm came loose. *Crack!* A leg popped off.
"Goodbye . . ." groaned Mr. Bizzo.

I thought this was going
to be fun, Stanley said
to himself. I think I
was wrong!

Finally, Stanley went to talk to Mr. Winger.

"Being star of the week has been awful," said Stanley.
"Nobody liked my favorite food. They laughed at my
favorite toy. I don't think I want to share any more."

"I know it has been challenging," said Mr. Winger. "But I
think it's really important that you finish what you start.
I can't wait to see what you share next."

When it was time for Stanley to share what he liked to do best, everyone sat quietly on the rug.

"I love to draw," Stanley whispered.

"This is going to be as good as that silly robot!" said Polly Seedeater. There was giggling.

Mr. Winger suggested that Stanley draw something.

Stanley froze.

His arms felt stiff, like tree branches.

He wished
he could
disappear.

All Stanley Birdbaum could draw
was a little curvy line.

"That's not what I meant
to do," he said.

"Stanley Birdbaum loves to draw noodles!" sang Polly.

There was laughing.

"Well . . . it *could* be a worm!" said Larry Finchfeather.

Stanley smiled at Larry and began to draw.
"Ta-da!" he announced. "Now it *is* a worm!"

"It's a *squiggle* drawing," someone shouted.
"And it's *great*!"

"Do another one!" said Larry Finchfeather.

Before Stanley could begin,
Polly marched right up

to the front of the room.

"Here's a squiggle," she said. "I bet you can't make anything out of *this*!"

Everyone was quiet.

Stanley stared at the squiggle.

After a few moments, he began to draw.

"How about a bird looking for lunch?"
Stanley said when he'd finished drawing.

Everyone clapped.
Polly Seedeater had nothing to say.

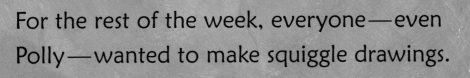

For the rest of the week, everyone—even
Polly—wanted to make squiggle drawings.

I thought this was going to be fun, Stanley said
to himself. I think I was right!